Flamingo plays bingo

Russell Punter

Illustrated by David Semple

A prize bingo game is just under way.
It's Flamingo's first time,
and she can't wait to play.

Flamingo's excited. "I'll try oh so hard, to match every number on my bingo card."

"We're beginning – get ready!"
is Elephant's call.

He spins his tombola
and picks the first ball.

"Twenty-two," he declares,
as he holds the ball high.

That's two
little ducks.

"Quack, quack!" players cry.

Flamingo feels puzzled.
Then Gazelle makes it clear.

Number 2 is a
duck shape.

"This is cool!" grins Flamingo.
"I've got twenty-two."

Number eight – one fat hippo.

Surprise Prize Bingo

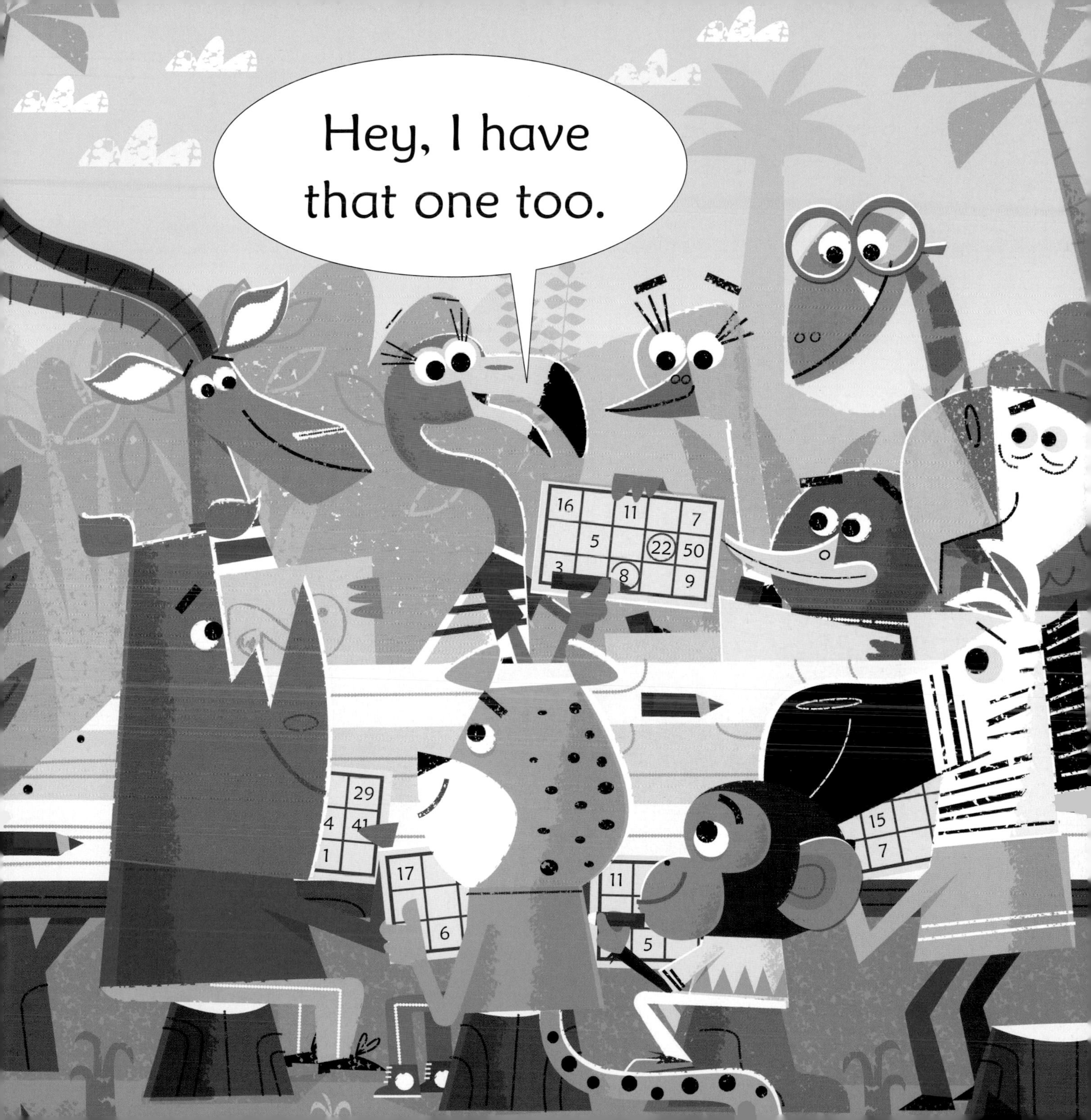
Hey, I have that one too.

"Achoo!" booms Elephant.

His jumbo-sized sneeze,
sees the next ball go zooming
up over the trees.

Down by the river,
there comes a shocked...

Duck flies to the skies
as he brings the ball back.

It lands with a thud,
in the mud right by Hippo.

"Oh no, it's a six,"
sighs unhappy Flamingo.

"Don't panic!" says Elephant.

"It goes *under* the number,
which means it's a nine!"

"Bingo!" cries Flamingo.

Gazelle brings her prize –
it's a pair of pink stilts.

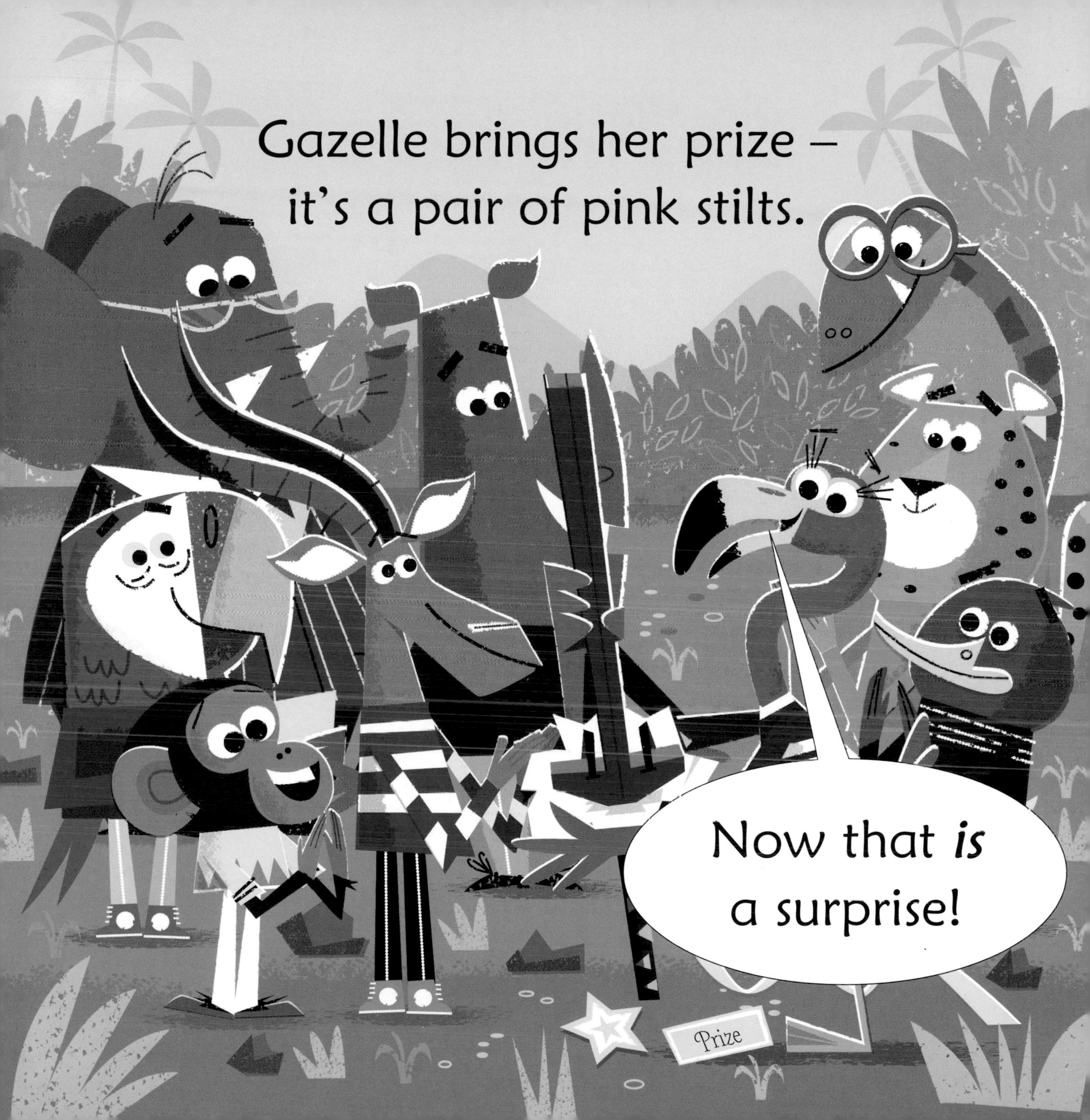

About phonics

Phonics is a method of teaching reading used extensively in today's schools. At its heart is an emphasis on identifying the *sounds* of letters, or combinations of letters, that are then put together to make words. These sounds are known as phonemes.

Starting to read

Learning to read is an important milestone for any child. The process can begin well before children start to learn letters and put them together to read words. The sooner children can discover books and enjoy stories and language, the better they will be prepared for reading themselves, first with the help of an adult and then independently.

You can find out more about phonics on the Usborne Very First Reading website, **www.usborne.com/veryfirstreading** (US readers go to **www.veryfirstreading.com**). Click on the **Parents** tab at the top of the page, then scroll down and click on **About synthetic phonics**.

Phonemic awareness

An important early stage in pre-reading and early reading is developing phonemic awareness: that is, listening out for the sounds within words. Rhymes, rhyming stories and alliteration are excellent ways of encouraging phonemic awareness.

In this story, your child will soon identify the *ing* sound, as in **flamingo** and **bingo**. Look out, too, for rhymes such as **call** – **ball** and **line** – **nine**.

Hearing your child read

If your child is reading a story to you, don't rush to correct mistakes, but be ready to prompt or guide if he or she is struggling. Above all, do give plenty of praise and encouragement.

Edited by Lesley Sims
Designed by Hope Reynolds

Reading consultants: Alison Kelly and Anne Washtell

With thanks to Harriet Punter

First published in 2018 by Usborne Publishing Ltd., Usborne House, 83-85 Saffron Hill, London EC1N 8RT, England.
www.usborne.com Copyright © 2018 Usborne Publishing Ltd.